.CLASSICS.
Illustrated®

Jack London
THE CALL OF THE WILD

essay by
Joshua Miller, M. Phil.
Columbia University

ACCLAIM BOOKS
STUDY GUIDE

The Call of the Wild
Originally published as Classics Illustrated no. 91

Art by Maurice del Bourgo
Adaption by Ken Fitch
Cover by Leonardo Manco

For Classics Illustrated Study Guides
computer recoloring by Twilight Graphics
editor: Madeleine Robins
assistant editor: Gregg Sanderson
design: Scott Friedlander

Dale-Chall R.L.: 7.6

ISBN 1-57840-042-2

Acclaim Books, New York, NY
Printed in the United States

GET OUT THAR, SPEETZ!

NOTHING REMAINED FOR BUCK BUT TO RECOVER HIS BONE. "THAT WAS FAIR OF FRANCOIS," HE DECIDED, AND THE HALF-BREED BEGAN TO RISE IN BUCK'S ESTIMATION . . .

DAY AND NIGHT, THE SHIP THROBBED TO THE TIRELESS PULSE OF THE PROPELLER. IT WAS APPARENT TO BUCK THAT THE WEATHER WAS STEADILY GROWING COLDER. AT LAST, ONE MORNING, THE "NARWHAL'S" PROPELLER WAS QUIET AND AN ATMOSPHERE OF EXCITEMENT PERVADED THE SHIP. BUCK KNEW THAT A CHANGE WAS AT HAND . . .

THEY HAD COME TO THE END OF A JOURNEY, TO SOME DESTINATION, AND ALL ABOUT THEM BLEW STRANGE WHITENESS, COLD AND SLIPPERY, THAT FELL LIKE RAIN, AND LAY LIKE A BLANKET UPON THE DECK AS THEY DISEMBARKED.

THE FIRST DAY AT DYEA BEACH WAS LIKE A NIGHTMARE. BUCK, COME FROM CIVILIZATION, HAD BEEN SUDDENLY THRUST AMONG SAVAGES . . . BOTH ANIMALS AND HUMANS. HE HAD EARLIER BEEN INTRODUCED TO THE LAW OF THE CLUB; HERE HE LEARNED THE LAW OF THE FANG. CURLY APPROACHED THE LEADER OF A PACK OF HUSKIES . . .

CURLY'S ADVANCE WAS FRIENDLY, HER TAIL WAGGING. THERE WAS NO WARNING -- ONLY A LEAP LIKE A FLASH, A METALLIC CLICK OF TEETH . . .

IN A MOMENT, THE PACK OF HUSKIES SURROUNDED THE COMBATANTS IN AN INTENT SILENT CIRCLE . . . CURLY RUSHED THE VICIOUS LEADER . . .

THE HUSKY MET CURLY'S RUSH WITH HIS CHEST IN A PECULIAR FASHION THAT TUMBLED HER OFF HER FEET . . .

HE NEVER REGAINED THEM. THIS WAS WHAT THE ONLOOKING HUSKIES HAD WAITED FOR . . . THEY CLOSED IN UPON HER, SNARLING AND YELPING, AND SHE WAS BURIED BENEATH THE BRISTLING MASS OF BODIES.

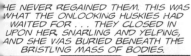

COME ON, PERRAULT. THESE DOGS EES GOT ONE OF OURS!

GET! GET!

IT HAD NOT TAKEN LONG. TWO MINUTES, PERHAPS, IN ALL. BUT THERE LAY CURLY, LIMP AND LIFELESS. NO FAIR PLAY. ONCE DOWN, THAT WAS THE END.

SPITZ, NEARBY, RAN OUT HIS TONGUE IN THE WAY HE HAD OF LAUGHING. FROM THAT MOMENT, BUCK HATED SPITZ WITH A BITTER AND DEATHLESS HATRED . . .

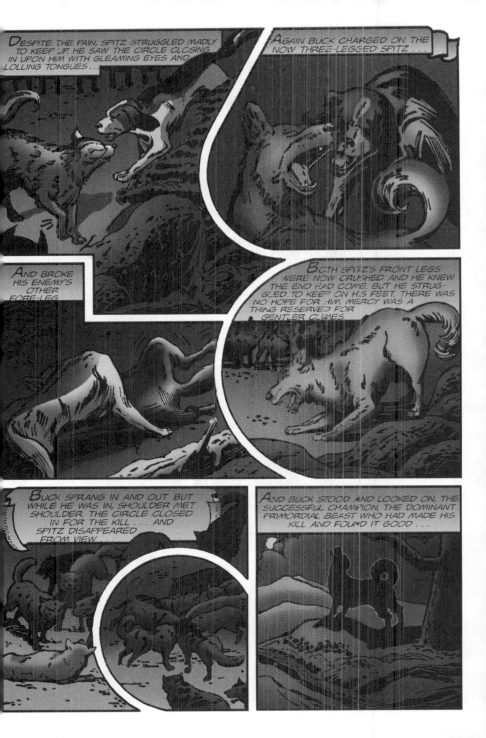

IN THE FALL OF THE YEAR, BUCK SAVED JOHN'S LIFE IN QUITE ANOTHER MANNER. THE THREE PARTNERS WERE GUIDING A LONG, NARROW POLING BOAT DOWN A BAD STRETCH OF RIVER...

LOOK OUT, JOHN! PY JINGO! ISS BAD RAPIDS!

BETTER CHECK IT WITH THE ROPE, HANS!

HEY!

BY JINGO, I PULL TOO HARD!

BUCK DOVE IN ON THE INSTANT. THORNTON WAS BEING SWIFTLY CARRIED DOWNSTREAM...

BUCK SOON OVERHAULED THORNTON. THORNTON GRABBED BUCK'S TAIL AND BUCK HEADED FOR THE BANK, SWIMMING WITH ALL HIS SPLENDID STRENGTH...

PROGRESS SHOREWARD WAS SLOW; PROGRESS DOWNSTREAM AMAZINGLY RAPID. FROM BELOW CAME THE FATAL ROARING WHERE THE WILD CURRENT WENT WILDER. THORNTON KNEW THAT THE SHORE WAS IMPOSSIBLE. HE CLUTCHED A SLIPPERY ROCK TOP WITH BOTH HANDS, RELEASING BUCK...

GO, BUCK! GO!

I GUESS JOHN'S A GONER! IF BUCK CAN'T MAKE IT, NOBODY CAN!

WE TRY ONE OTHER THING, MAYBE!

IN THOSE DREAM-MEMORIES, HE RECALLED THE WILD URGES THAT MADE SENSES ALERT. THEN HE WOULD REMEMBER THE THRILL OF KILLING OTHER WILD THINGS . . .

ALTHOUGH THE MEN DID NOT FIND A LOST MINE, THEY DID COME UPON A SHALLOW STREAM IN A BROAD VALLEY WHERE GOLD SHOWED LIKE YELLOW BUTTER ACROSS THE BOTTOM OF THE WASHING PAN. THEY SOUGHT NO FARTHER . . .

ONE NIGHT, BUCK SPRANG FROM HIS SLEEP WITH A START. FROM THE FOREST CAME A CALL, MANY-NOTED, DISTINCT AND DEFINITE AS NEVER BEFORE. A HOWL, YET UNLIKE THAT OF ANY HUSKY DOG . . .

BUCK SPRANG THROUGH THE SLEEPING CAMP IN SWIFT SILENCE, DASHED THROUGH THE WOODS. THOUGH THE SOUND OF THE HOWL WAS NEW, IT WAS AS IF HE HAD KNOWN IT ALWAYS . . .

CAUTIOUSLY, BUCK FOLLOWED HIS INSTINCTS. THEN, SUDDENLY, THE HOWLING STOPPED. BUCK FACED A TIMBER WOLF. THE WOLF FLED AT THE SIGHT OF BUCK, WHO WAS MUCH LARGER AND HEAVIER . . .

BUCK FOLLOWED, WITH WILD LEAPINGS, TO OVERTAKE THE WOLF. WHEN CORNERED, THE WOLF PREPARED FOR THE EXPECTED ATTACK, BUT NONE CAME. THEN THE WOLF WOULD AGAIN DASH OFF AT THE FIRST OPPORTUNITY . . .

IN THE END, BUCK'S PERSISTENCE WAS REWARDED. THE WOLF, FINDING NO HARM WAS INTENDED, SNIFFED NOSES . . .

AFTER SOME TIME, THE WOLF STARTED OFF AGAIN IN A MANNER THAT SHOWED PLAINLY THAT BUCK WAS TO FOLLOW.

SUDDENLY, BUCK REMEMBERED JOHN THORNTON AND HE TURNED BACK ABRUPTLY. THE WOLF BEGAN ONCE MORE TO HOWL, BUT BUCK DID NOT LOOK BACK.

BUT BUCK HAD THE BLOOD-LONGING AND IT HAD BECOME STRONGER EACH DAY. ON THE WAY BACK, HE CAME SUDDENLY UPON A MOOSE HERD...

HE SOUGHT OUT A HUGE BULL OF VICIOUS TEMPER AND DOGGED HIM UNTIL THE OTHERS OF THE HERD LEFT THEIR BROTHER MOOSE AND JOURNEYED ON THEIR WAY.

FOR FOUR DAYS, BUCK WORRIED THE BIG BULL, ALLOWING HIM NO TIME FOR FOOD OR WATER OR SLEEP, UNTIL AT LAST... AT THE END OF THE FOURTH DAY...

FOR A DAY AND A NIGHT, BUCK REMAINED BY THE KILL, EATING AND SLEEPING. THEN, RESTED AND REFRESHED, HE TURNED HIS FACE TOWARD CAMP AND JOHN THORNTON, BUT AS HE NEARED CAMP, HE WAS OPPRESSED WITH A SENSE OF CALAMITY HAPPENING, IF IT WERE NOT CALAMITY ALREADY HAPPENED. HE PROCEEDED WITH MORE SPEED AND GREATER CAUTION . . .

AS BUCK SLID ALONG WITH THE OBSCURENESS OF A GLIDING SHADOW, HIS NOSE WAS JERKED SUDDENLY TO THE SIDE AS THOUGH A POSITIVE FORCE HAD GRIPPED AND PULLED IT. HE FOLLOWED THE SCENT INTO A THICKET AND FOUND NIG . . . DEAD . . .

BELLYING FORWARD TO THE EDGE OF THE CLEARING, HE FOUND HANS, FEATHERED WITH ARROWS LIKE A PORCUPINE. FROM WITHIN THE CAMP CAME THE STRANGE SOUNDS OF THE YEEHAT INDIANS IN A WAR DANCE . . .

FOR A MOMENT, BUCK LOOKED ON IN SILENCE. THEN, FOR THE LAST TIME IN HIS LIFE, HE ALLOWED PASSION TO USURP CUNNING AND REASON AND IT WAS BECAUSE OF HIS GREAT LOVE FOR JOHN THORNTON THAT HE LOST HIS HEAD. THE YEEHATS HEARD A FEARFUL ROAR AND SAW RUSHING UPON THEM AN ANIMAL THE LIKE OF WHICH THEY HAD NEVER SEEN BEFORE . . .

IT WAS BUCK, A LIVE HURRICANE OF FURY, HURLING HIMSELF UPON THEM IN A FRENZY TO DESTROY. THERE WAS NO WITHSTANDING HIM. HE PLUNGED INTO THEIR MIDST, RENDING, DESTROYING!

TRULY BUCK WAS A FIEND INCARNATE. AND THE YEEHATS, TRYING TO SPEAR HIM IN CLOSE QUARTERS, SPEARED ONE ANOTHER INSTEAD...

PANIC SEIZED THE YEEHATS AND THEY FLED IN TERROR TO THE WOODS, BUCK AT THEIR HEELS, DRAGGING THEM DOWN AS THEY RACED THROUGH THE TREES...

SOON WEARYING OF THE PURSUIT, BUCK RETURNED TO THE DESOLATE CAMP. HE FOUND PETE IN HIS BLANKETS, KILLED IN THE FIRST MOMENT OF SURPRISE. THORNTON'S DESPERATE STRUGGLE WAS FRESH-WRITTEN ON THE EARTH, AND BUCK SCENTED EVERY DETAIL OF IT DOWN TO THE EDGE OF A DEEP POOL. BY THE EDGE LAY SKEET, FAITHFUL TO THE LAST. THE POOL ITSELF EFFECTUALLY HID WHAT IT CONTAINED ... AND IT CONTAINED JOHN THORNTON...

FOR A DAY, BUCK BROODED BY THE POOL, OR ROAMED RESTLESSLY ABOUT THE CAMP. HE KNEW JOHN THORNTON WAS DEAD AND IT LEFT A GREAT VOID IN HIM SOMEWHAT AKIN TO HUNGER, BUT A VOID WHICH ACHED AND ACHED...

AT TIMES, WHEN HE PASSED THE BODY OF AN INDIAN, HE FORGOT THE PAIN OF IT. AND WITHIN HIM GREW A GREAT SENSE OF SELF-PRIDE. HE HAD KILLED MAN, THE NOBLEST GAME OF ALL, AND HE HAD KILLED IN THE FACE OF CLUB AND FANG...

BUCK WALKED TO THE CENTER OF THE OPEN SPACE AND LISTENED. IT WAS THE CALL OF THE WILD, AND AS NEVER BEFORE, BUCK WAS READY TO OBEY. JOHN THORNTON WAS DEAD. THE LAST TIE WAS BROKEN. MAN AND THE CLAIMS OF MAN NO LONGER BOUND HIM . . .

NIGHT CAME, AND A FULL MOON ROSE HIGH IN THE SKY. BUCK HEARD AGAIN THE WILD HOWLS OF THE TIMBER WOLF . . .

HUNTING THEIR LIVING MEAT, THE WOLF PACK HAD AT LAST INVADED BUCK'S VALLEY . . .

INTO THE CLEARING, WHERE THE MOONLIGHT STREAMED, THEY POURED IN A SILVERY FLOOD, AND IN THE CENTER OF THE CLEARING STOOD BUCK, MOTIONLESS AS A STATUE, WAITING FOR THEM . . .

THEY WERE AWED, SO STILL AND LARGE HE STOOD . . .

THE CALL OF THE WILD
JACK LONDON

Set deep in the frigid tundra of Alaska and the Canadian Yukon, *The Call of the Wild* portrays both the cruelty and the generosity between humans and all creatures in the face of freezing death. Filled with narrow escapes, exciting chases, and heroic efforts to save lives, *Call* is the best known work by the one of the most widely read American writers. The terms of London's narrative—the regression from "civilization" to the primitive "wild"—may sound somewhat old fashioned today, but his characters and their adventures remain as harrowing now as they were when they first appeared in 1903. Unlike many of the writers of his time, London reverses many of the presumptions regarding society and solitude. In *Call*, the wild or the "savage" element is the most immediate and genuine quality. "Civilized," here, is simply another term for the artificial or inauthentic.

The Author

Parts of London's early childhood remain obscure, but we know that he was born on January 12, 1876, in San Francisco. His mother, Flora Wellman, was a spiritualist and music teacher who bore only one child. London's father—and Flora's common-law husband—was probably William Henry Chaney, a traveling astrologist who fled when he learned of her pregnancy. Flora Wellman married a Civil War veteran named John London months after giving birth. Her son was given his father's name at birth, but Flora renamed him after his stepfather: John Griffith London.

Jack London grew up while his family bounced between Oakland poorhouses and farms on the San Francisco Bay. His parents' get-rich-quick plans rarely panned out and the family hovered on the brink of poverty for most of his childhood. As a young boy, Jack took jobs selling newspapers, canning fish, and sweeping in a saloon. By the time he was fifteen, Jack was illegally pirating oysters on the Bay. Working in humiliating (and sometimes criminal) employment helped to galvanize London's life-long disgust for wage-labor and all forms of capitalism.

At seventeen, he took his first sea voyage aboard the sealer *Sofia Sutherland* for seven months in the Bering Sea. From his experiences sealing (the bloody job itself as well as a fierce typhoon off the coast of Japan), London published some of his earliest writing.

In July of 1897, London joined his brother-in-law in the Klondike gold rush. They spent the winter in a cabin where Jack developed scurvy, a disease brought on by poor nutrition. He returned to California the following summer and, while the trip was not a major success in terms of gold, much of London's early fiction drew on his time in the Yukon Territory. The frozen lands that he saw during this eleven-month stay formed the basis of the author's fiction and his literary philosophy for the rest of his life.

In the aftermath of the Klondike trip, London published three collections of short stories in three years (1900-1902). *The Call of the Wild,* published in 1903, was what we might call his "breakthrough" work.

Writing quickly, as he did throughout his life, London wrote the story in just under two months (December-January, 1902 3), according to his own records. He seems to have been unaware that he was writing a classic; in letter he refers to the book as simply "my dog story." But the success of the work was immediate and sensational. *Call* brought London—to this point a little known author—an international audience.

Many of London's contemporaries remarked on the novella' "thrilling scenes" of violence and suspense. *The Argonaut* described it as an example of "the new romance" and "the poetry of the living world's real, not its imagined, history." The *Atlantic Monthly* suggested that it "is a story altogether untouched by bookishness" and is filled with action. Another reviewer, in the *Reader*, called the book "cruel" and "often relentless reading" because "we feel at times the blood lashing in our faces" from the savagery of the story. It might be worth keeping in mind, however, that this criticism is actually a hidden compliment: only a writer

Historical Context: The Klondike Gold Rush

When London wrote *The Call of the Wild*, he could assume that most, if not all, of his readers would be quite familiar with the sites and events of the recent gold rush. During the late 1890s, magazines, newspapers, and journals ran article after article about the northwestern region where the Canadian province of British Columbia and the Northwest Territories met Alaska. Publishers also printed huge numbers of books with intricate maps and illustrations. Today, however, readers are unlikely to recognize the names of communities that have not existed for a half-century or more. And the feverish excitement surrounding the 1897 rush may be hard to imagine a century after the fact.

Explorers and prospectors had traversed Alaska, the Canadian Yukon, and the Northwest Territories for decades before the rush, searching for what London calls "a yellow metal." Although minor gold strikes took place earlier, the flood began in earnest in August of 1896 when a small group of prospectors found the riverbeds of the Yukon and Klondike rivers rich with the precious element. Within weeks, Rabbit Creek (appropriately renamed "Bonanza Creek"!) and nearby Eldorado Creek were the sites of the last major gold rush.

BUCK COULD NOT READ THE NEWSPAPERS OR HE WOULD HAVE KNOWN THAT TROUBLE WAS BREWING FOR STRONG DOGS IN THAT YEAR OF 1897... THE YEAR WHEN GOLD HAD BEEN DISCOVERED IN ALASKA THAT NIGHT, MANUEL AND BUCK WENT FOR WHAT BUCK IMAGINED WAS MERELY A STROLL...

Early explorers and historians guess that approximately fifteen thousand people were searching for gold in the Yukon valley by 1896. But by mid-1897, over one hundred thousand people poured into the area seeking to make their fortune.

Most of those bound for the Klondike area traveled to newly formed towns on the southern Alaskan coast. Dyea, where London's characters land, was one such town. From this southern point, explorers had to travel over the Coastal Mountains and wind their way over (often partially) frozen lakes and the treacherous Yukon River before reaching their destination: Dawson City, Yukon.

who evokes utterly realistic scenes can be accused of making his or her readers "feel" the struggles within the text.

In addition to writing continuously, London was a Socialist candidate for mayor of Oakland twice (1901 and 1905, both losses), a journalist covering the Russo-Japanese war in Japan and Korea (1904), and a lecturer all over the U.S. After he'd separated from his wife of only a few years (whom he had never loved), they divorced in 1905. The very next day he married his love, Charmian Kittridge. The publicity from all of these activities, his ceaseless writing, and the brutal adventures in his fiction gave London the public image of an invincible superman. But he was never able to top his early successes. His later literary and physical challenges often ended in failure and financial ruin.

In 1907, London and Charmian set sail for a voyage around the world in a boat that he built himself, the *Snark*. After many delays (including the devastating 1906 San Francisco earthquake!), they traveled through Hawaii, the Marquesas Islands, and Tahiti. But by the time they reached Australia, in 1908, his health had utterly collapsed. He was hospitalized and abandoned his ship in the Solomon Islands. He returned to California the next year, after a lengthy stay in Sydney, Australia.

London's final seven years were filled with turbulent activity and debilitating sicknesses. He bega building his mansion, the stone "Wolf House" that he claimed woul survive for "a thousand years," but burned down in 1913. His alcoholism (which he portrayed starkly *John Barleycorn*, published in 1913 contributed to his failing health, eve as he continued to write prodigious. Following a strict routine of daily writing, London managed to publis a novel every year except one for fourteen years. Remarkably, he com posed *eighteen* novels during that period! Altogether he wrote more than fifty books in twenty years.

Suffering from various diseases and deteriorating health, London took long trips to Hawaii. Rather than recuperating there, his despondency simply increased. He fell into a coma that may have resul ed from an intentional overdose of his medications and he died, at the age of forty, on November 22, 1916

Characters

London's intense, urgent writing style lends *Call* the sense that somethin important is happening at every minute. It is a measur of his artistry that readers often feel themselves drawn deeply into the lives of his characters, even though the most important figures in this

The Role of Dogs in the Gold Rush

London's use of dogs in *Call* is far from accidental. Throughout the northern lands, dogs play crucial roles in the lives of inhabitants. During the Klondike Gold Rush, dogs were especially important and, hence, London's focus tells us a great deal about both the time and the place of the story.

In the intense cold of the area, humans could not possibly walk the great distances between communities (for example between Dyea Beach, Alaska, and Dawson City, in the Canadian Yukon, the route that Buck and his mates travel) and carry all the necessary supplies. As couriers, Perrault and François have sacks of dispatches to deliver (in addition to their food, shelter, and personal articles). But, by 1897, neither could machines do the job. Even the great railroads, spreading throughout Canada and the U.S., were unable (at this time) to penetrate the hazardous mountains and across the icy terrain.

Finally, other animals (even those used for transportation in more southerly climates, such as the horse and mule) proved inadequate since they couldn't gain traction in the snow to pull carts or sleds and wouldn't be able to eat the little food that the environment would allow. The trail provided little vegetation, but quantities of fish, rabbits, and other living food. Dogs were the only animals whose adaptability and strength could be applied to the difficult conditions. On his trip to the Yukon, London took note of the great regard that his companions had for the dogs that made their existence there possible. London was so impressed himself by the abilities of some of the dogs and their fierceness that he modeled Buck on a particular dog in Dawson City (aptly named "Jack).

IT WAS NO LIGHT RUNNING NOW. THIS WAS THE MAIL TRAIN. IT WAS HEAVY TOIL EACH DAY WITH A HEAVY LOAD BEHIND, CARRYING WORD FROM THE WORLD TO THE MEN WHO SOUGHT GOLD UNDER THE SHADOW OF THE NORTH POLE...

work are not humans. London gives each of the dogs in this book distinctive qualities, personalities much like humans. He makes these characteristics vivid in the constant activity of the dogs.

Buck

This is possibly the most famous dog in U.S. literature. Buck is the noble, graceful, manicured housedog who is unjustly sold into the slavery of the Alaskan gold rush. As he meets new challenges (harsh winters, brutal masters, deceitful mates), Buck overcomes them and earns the respect of those around him, both animals and humans. **It is precisely this "adaptability, his capacity to adjust himself to changing conditions" that sets Buck apart from all the other dogs; he has a shrewd inventiveness and intelligence that mark him as a leader.** His imagination is "a quality that made for greatness."

But as Buck becomes the master of his domain, he also sheds more and more of the trappings of humanity and civilization. His first few weeks and months at work are filled with painful lessons (both large and small) that keep him alive under conditions he never knew existed. He learns how to dig himself a warm hole underneath the snow to sleep during the night. After his first kill, his sled-masters notice his "instant and terrible transformation" from a friendly companion into "a thing of the wild."

London uses Buck to illustrate his theory that "the wild" lurks deep within all living creatures and that the chaos and viciousness of nature is much closer to "true" life than any part of civilization. Although Buck lived every minute of his first four years of life as a sheltered, nurtured, pampered housedog, after just a few days in the frozen tundra, he intuitively benefits from knowledge that only previous generations of dogs could have. He adapts to life as a sled-dog largely by, as London puts it, "harking back through his own life to the lives of his forebears." Even as he describes it, London cannot entirely decide himself whether this process by which Buck becomes the leader of his peers is a "development (or regression)."

HIGHLY AS FRANCOIS HAD VALUED BUCK, HE FOUND, WHILE THE DAY WAS YET YOUNG, THAT HE HAD UNDERVALUED HIM. AT A BOUND, BUCK TOOK UP HIS DUTIES OF LEADERSHIP. FOR QUICK THINKING AND ACTING, HE SHOWED HIMSELF SUPERIOR EVEN TO SPITZ . . .

Buck becomes more and more "primitive" as the story continues, but this does not necessarily signify something negative. In fact, London thinks of the primitive as a natural and entirely genuine quality. Finally, Buck struggles between his own unbending loyalty to a kind human and his innate desire to roam freely without any attachments. He never has to make that choice, since his beloved, final friend, John

Thornton is killed by the Yeehats. Saddened by the loss, **Buck drops his last tie to any group or society and answers "the call of the wild," joining (and, of course, leading) a pack of wolves for the rest of his life.**

Manuel

The gardener's assistant at Buck's original home, Judge Miller's estate in the Santa Clara Valley. Manuel's unfortunate weakness is gambling and—even more unfortunately—he isn't very good at it. Deep in debt, Manuel secretly sells Buck to a middleman in the sled-dog trade. One literary critic, Daniel Dyer, notes that an Oakland councilman named Walter G. Manuel may be the source of this name. During the 1890s, Councilman Manuel was a well-known opponent of the Chinese lottery. Ironically, London seems to have turned the politician who was recognized for fighting gambling into the character whose weakness for gambling takes Buck away from his plush life in California.

The Man in the Red-Sweater

Although he makes only a very brief appearance in the story, the red sweatered man and his club give Buck his first lesson in life on his own. At first, Buck is indignant at being kidnapped, **but this "dogbreaker" coolly**

crushes him and gives him "his

London's Sources for *The Call of the Wild*

The source that critics tend to give for *Call* is London himself: his trip to the Yukon, his lifelong pursuit of adventure, his fascination with stories of survival. But London had important literary influences as well. His fiction, alternatively "realism" and "romance," was shaped by his early love of reading (he would borrow other people's library cards in order to check out as many books as possible). In an autobiographical book, he recalls that he read almost continuously: "I read mornings, afternoons, and nights. I read in bed, I read at table, I read as I walked to and from school, and I read at recess while the other boys were playing." London credits the British author Rudyard Kipling with early influence on him. Kipling's animal stories undoubtedly play into London's narration from Buck's point-of-view. A reviewer in the *Atlantic Monthly* even called London "the American Kipling."

Another author whose literary views were especially useful for London was the French author and social critic, Emile Zola. Zola was one of the major advocates of "naturalism," showing the daily life of characters exactly as it happened to them. Like London, Zola was interested in Darwin's theories of evolution. Zola's writings were controversial in that they described sex frankly and openly as the result of physical needs and desires. London was fascinated by this attempt to show the importance of human instincts and he would use similar techniques in regard to the dogs that populate his fiction. In *Call*, London continually focuses on the instincts and actions of his characters, rather than on a longer and more complex plot.

One influence for which London had to answer publicly was the genre of the true-adventure story. Some close readers found that London had taken information from a book published in 1902 by Egerton R. Young called *My Dogs in the Northland*. This work of non-fiction was Young's account of his own trip north. Having been charged with plagiarism, London responded that he would "plead guilty" to the charge of using information from Young's book (with the author's knowledge) in his own. But London refused to call this plagiarism, since "fiction-writers have always considered actual experiences of life to be a lawful field for exploitation." London defended this form of "exploitation" as simply the usual manner in which authors turn the events around them into works of fantasy.

ntroduction to the reign of primitive law," the rule of strength. Although beaten badly, Buck is humble enough to recognize that he cannot compete with the man's club and he retreats before being fully broken.

London based this character on the numerous Seattle dog-trainers whose services were in much demand during the Gold Rush. These "trainers" would often sell the dogs on the streets of Seattle to those on their way to the Yukon.

Perrault

The French-Canadian government courier who recognizes Buck immediately as "one in ten t'ousand" dogs and buys him from the man in the red sweater. Perrault's bravery and dedication to his job command Buck's respect. Perrault puts the safety and health of the dogs ahead even of his own as he tests thinly-frozen ice himself before letting the sled go across. When the team runs into a sheer cliff, Perrault refuses to waste time by circling around it. **Instead, he hoists the dogs over it, one by one, until they are all across.** As his first master in the wild, Buck develops a relationship with Perrault of respect, though not love.

François

The second French-Canadian courier is a "black-faced giant" and a "half-breed" whose fairness and calm kindness match his partner's. The mixed ancestry to which London presumably refers is that of Caucasian and Native American. The term "half-breed" was a common derogatory expression, but it was also one of the official categories of prisoners during this period (the others included "civilians," "indians," and "lunatics"). The two Canadian couriers may indeed have carried important dispatches since the federal government was then worried that a massive rush of explorers to the Yukon could result in widespread starvation (there was little natural food there).

Government officials sent official documents to and from Dawson City in order to work out arrangements for famine or other catastrophies.

THAT IS WHY PERRAULT WAS MADE GOVERNMENT DISPATCHER. NOTHING DAUNTED HIM. ONCE, BLOCKED BY A GLACIER BARRIER, HE CLIMBED TO THE TOP OF THE ICY HILL AND LIFTED THE DOGS, SLED AND FRANCOIS UP, ONE BY ONE...

YOU ALL RIGHT, PERRAULT?

IS OKAY. GET OTHER DOG READY FOR LIFT.

Spitz

The lead dog of Perrault and François's sled-team. A big, white dog from a group of Arctic islands north of Norway. Whiteness, in the context of the snowy terrain of the Yukon, contains an interesting ambiguity. While white has historically been used to symbolize "purity," it has a very different meaning here. A white dog can almost disappear against the equally white background of snow and ice. Spitz's white coloring is a form of Northern camouflage that makes him even more treacherous.

BUT EVEN WHILE BUCK WAS DEFENDING HIMSELF, THE TREACHEROUS SPITZ WOULD NOT MISS AN OPPORTUNITY TO STRIKE . . .

Spitz appears friendly, but he guards his position as the leader fiercely. Cold and calculating, he recognizes Buck as a threat almost immediately and bides his time until he gets his chance to fight him. **Their first skirmish ends prematurely when the entire camp is attacked by a pack of starving wolves,** but their second struggle proves decisive. Spitz, never one to miss an opportunity for an advantage, attacks Buck by surprise during a rabbit chase. Spitz's superior fighting skills and experience help him to trick Buck, but ultimately the stronger, more creative dog prevails.

"Spitz" (German for "pointed") was also a common name for wide, strong dogs with pointed ears.

Curly

Buck's mate in the cages of the man with the red sweater, Curly is the female Newfoundland that Perrault buys along with Buck. Curly's death, early in the story, provides Buck with some of his first lessons about life in the wild: never drop one's guard, and if one fights, it is to the death. Curly's inexperience rapidly gets her in trouble with another dog and when they square off to fight, the husky overturns her. As soon as Curly hits the ground, she is mauled by the circle of dogs around them: "So that was the way. No fair play. Once down, that was the end of you. Well, he ould see to it that he never went own." Buck's ability to learn not nly from his own mistakes, but om those of other dogs shows his nique adaptability to new situaons. He learns the laws of the ild largely by watching others nd learning from them.

Dave and Sol-leks

Two more sled dogs that Buck joins under the command of errault and François. Both dogs re quiet, sullen characters who vant nothing to do with the others. They do their work nd stay away from he rest of the ack. Buck (and ve readers) meets Dave on board the hip to Alaska. Buck notices mmediately that all he desired was o be left alone, and further, that here would be trouble if he were ot." Sol-leks's name means "the ngry One" in Chinook, a lanuage of northwestern Native americans. This one-eyed dog imilarly "asked nothing, gave othing, [and] expected nothing." The two dogs play very minor oles in the CI adaptation, but they re important as contrasts to both he leaders (Spitz and later Buck) nd the followers among the dogs.

Considering that survival requires a unified team effort, it is worth noting that Dave and Sol-leks participate and yet stand apart from the rest of the group.

Hal, Charles, and Mercedes

London portrays the three would-be explorers as vastly unprepared and overmatched by the elements of nature. Mercedes, Charles's wife and Hal's sister, is an unusual character for London (female characters in his fiction are generally not this poorly suited to their task), but women were not uncommon during the historical event. Local newspapers heralded the fact that the Rush brought large numbers of women to the Yukon. "The Women's Klondike Expedition Syndicate" was even formed to recognize some of the most prominent female explorers on the scene.

Like Mercedes, Hal and Charles are "manifestly out of place," as the narrator puts it, in the harsh Yukon climate. **With little knowledge of the terrain and no understanding of the sled-dogs, Hal and Charles fail miserably.** Their end, drowning in a par-

AFTER A LAYOVER TO DISPOSE OF MATERIAL, HAL AND CHARLES SHOPPED AROUND AND RETURNED WITH SIX ADDITIONAL DOGS WITHOUT REALIZING THAT THE SLED WOULD NOT BE LARGE ENOUGH TO HAUL FOOD FOR THAT MANY. THEN THEY STARTED AGAIN...

WE'RE REALLY DOING THINGS UP RIGHT, CHARLES. FOURTEEN! THE MOST THE OTHERS HAVE IS EIGHT

CHARLES! HAL! WAIT A MOMENT!

tially frozen section of the Yukon, was not unusual during the Rush.

John Thornton

London probably based the name of his most sympathetic character on one of his companions. When he left the Klondike in 1898, London floated down the Yukon River with a man named John

BUCK AT LAST HAD FOUND, IN JOHN THORNTON, A KINDNESS AND LOVE THAT HE HAD NEVER KNOWN BEFORE, EVEN IN THE SOUTHLAND. IN RETURN, HE ADORED THE MASTER WITH A FIERCE DEVOTION...

Thor*son*. In *Call*, John Thornton saves Buck from imminent death at the hands of Hal and his club. **Thornton is Buck's last and most intimate human contact.** Buck's loyalty to Thornton is tested by his impulse toward the "call of the wild." Thornton's death at the hands of the Yeehats erases Buck's dilemma. It is worth noting that London invented the Yeehats (since he was usually careful to use historical people and events in his fiction). Legends of fierce Native American tribes circulated among the visitors to the Klondike, but incidents of actual violence were extremely rare.

"Black" Burton

A minor character who threatens John Thornton and unknowingly bears the fury of Buck's revenge. London likely means for this incident to show the extent of Buck's loyalty to Thornton, and to compare this loyalty with his simultaneous desire for life on his own in the wilderness. But Burton's nickname was not necessarily picked randomly. A plethora of nicknames emerged from the Klondike Gold Rush and African Americans were often called "Black." One African-American bartender in a nearby Alaskan city went by the name of "Black Bill." And "Black Mike's Bar" was a sandbar named for "the color of the man who located it," according to an explorer.

Darwinism and Londonism: Survival of the Fittest

Charles Darwin published *On the Origin of Species* in 1859 and the major tenets of Evolution have been linked to his name ever since. Darwin claimed that over the thousands of years of life on Earth, millions of species of living creatures compete for natural resources and, thus, only those most fit to survive, do survive. Darwin's arguments were enormously influential (as well as controversial) and continue to spark debate today. In the years preceding London's composition

The Call of the Wild, sociolo-
sts, scientists, and pseudoscien-
ts were hotly debating the impli-
tions of "Social Darwinism," the
ea that Darwin's thesis regarding
ecies could be true for groups of
man beings as well. Social
arwinists would argue that some
mans are superior to (or fitter
an) others and these individuals
ould rule over society. In ways
at are obvious with the benefit
historical hindsight, these prin-
ples created dangerous rationales
r oppression based on race, eth-
city, socioeconomic class, gen-
r, nationality, and even religion.

Jack London
as impressed
ough by the
portance of
arwin's book to
ing a copy of *On
e Origin of
ecies* with him on
s 1896-7 trip to
e Klondike. But
was no doctrinaire follower of
ocial (or any other form of)
arwinism. In *Call*, he defines the
eaning of "fittest" as going
ainst the process of evolution.
he novella tells the tale of regres-
on or backward movement from
e state of civilization to the state
nature, "the wild." But this pas-
ge is not—according to the
thor's values and concerns—

regressive. It is, in fact, progres-
sive. The call (or calling) that
takes Buck-the-housedog and turns
him into a creature of the Wild
gives him insights into life that he
could never see before.

**Throughout the work,
London hints at Buck's "early,"
"distant," and "primeval" memories.** These are not Buck's personal memories (remember, he is
born and bred in domesticity), but
his instinctive connection to the
lives of his ancestors. London
invokes Buck's "other world" as a
hint to both the Darwinian process
of evolution that made him and the

sense in which that former life (in
the Wild) remains within him,
awaiting release. In this way, Buck
"was older than the days he had
seen and the breaths he had drawn.
He linked the past with the present, and the eternity behind him
throbbed through him in a mighty
rhythm."

After a period of months in
the Yukon pulling sleds, Buck has

forgotten his puppyhood in California. In contrast to earlier moments in the narrative, London makes a point of remarking that Buck "was not homesick." Instead, he recalls an earlier era:

Far more potent were the memories of his heredity that gave things he had never seen before a seeming familiarity; the instincts (which were but the memories of his ancestors become habits) which had lapsed in later days, and still later, in him, quickened and became alive again.

London purposefully phrases Buck's instinctual actions as "the memories of his ancestors become habits" to emphasize the renewed links between Buck and his predecessors. London gives Darwin a creative spin by ascribing intergenerational memory and hibernating instinct to a being that individually could not have experienced them before.

London is at his most Darwinian at the conclusion of *Call*. The Yeehats notice "a change in the breed of timber wolves" around them, some time after John Thornton's death prompts Buck to forsake human contact entirely. Not only have the wolves' colors changed, they have become more ferocious, brave, and imaginative. This description suggests that Buck's

move to the Wild has consequences beyond his own life. London's point is that Buck's presence among the wolves has actually changed the "breed" of wolf. Through a Darwinian process of natural selection, Buck's characteristics spread through the group and alter its very nature. As for Buck himsel he rules what London calls "the younger world" of living creatures.

Civilization vs. The Wild

Although critics general read *Call* as a story of decisive movement from a state of civiliz tion to one of savagery, Buck remains—at all points of his life a hybrid of both worlds. On the one hand, he has an instinctual "savagery" within him (London careful to point out) from the beginning; on the other hand, he maintains some elements of his (so-called) "civilized" manner (imagination, creativity, intelligence) until the end. When Buc fights Spitz, he wounds him by inventing his own way of fightin Unlike all the other dogs in the pack, Buck's "greatness" rests o his ability to improvise solutions for dangerous problems.

It might help to think of the story's central conflict in way other than simply between civi-

Within the comic panels:

THE DAYS THAT FOLLOWED WERE HARD TO BEAR, BUT BUCK LEARNED QUICKLY AND DID NOT LIKE THE WORK. HE LEARNED MANY THINGS ABOUT TEAM WORK AND ABOUT SURVIVAL...

HE LEARNED TO SLEEP CURLED WARMLY UNDER THE SNOW...

TO TAKE HIS PLACE IN HARNESS WITHOUT EARNING THE DISPLEASURE OF HIS MATES...

...AND HE LEARNED TO BE SLY, FOR IN THE WILD, SOMETIMES, ONLY THE WISEST AND SLYEST ARE THE ONES THAT SURVIVE.

...ed society and the wilderness. ...fact, London presents the two as ...newhat similar. Just as Buck ...esumably) had to learn how to ...have at Judge Miller's estate, he ...o has to *learn* how to act in ...der to survive the frozen Wild of ...: Yukon.

London makes much of ...ck's instincts for the Wild, but ...ck could never survive on his ...'n simply on the basis of his ...ate, ancestral memories. **Before ... begins to sense his kinship ...th life in the wilderness, he ...s to learn how to sleep at night ...y digging a hole under the ...ow) and how to fight with ...er dogs (unfairly).** This ...mesticated housedog has to ...rn his lessons slowly and ...infully. London does not allow ...ck to suddenly understand all ...: necessities of survival in a ...sh. Buck learns by watching the ...er dogs and occasionally mak-...; mistakes (such as approaching ...-leks on his blind side, a small

event that doesn't appear in the Classics Illustrated adaptation).

One could read the progress of Buck's story (rather than from society to the Wild) as one of Buck learning to live more independently within another kind of social system. Toward the end of the novella, the author makes the important point that—as a wolf-dog, the leader of a pack of wild creatures—Buck is both a member of their group and apart from them. The narrator tells us that "there is one visitor" to their valley, "of which the Yeehats do not know." He is an enormous wolf who *crosses alone from the smiling timber land and comes down into an open space among the trees. . . . Here he muses for a time, howling once, long and mournfully, ere he departs.*

But he is still a leader and a member of the wolves' pack. The narrator acknowledges this as well: "But he is not always alone. . . . he may be seen running at the head of the pack through the pale moonlight." Furthermore, Buck's presence could not affect the coloring and the attitudes of the wolves without his being an integral part of their society.

Ultimately, London sets up the conclusion of the novel as a choice that Buck will have to make. Torn between the appeal of the wolves' "call of the wild" and his love for John Thornton, he will have to sacrifice one for the other. Considering his growing impatience with Thornton and his increasing fascination with the wolves, it seems plausible to argue that Buck would choose to live with the wolves. But London takes this decision out of Buck's hands (paws) and makes it for him. The Yeehats kill Thornton before Buck makes his choice; this act resolves the dilemma before Buck has the chance to decide.

Anthropomorphism: Do These Dogs Really Think and Feel What London Suggests?

The problem with writing a novel from a dog's perspective is that it's impossible not to give the dog human characteristics. Giving human qualities to a non-human is called "anthropomorphism," and many readers find that London's dogs have personalities too similar to those of humans to be believable as dogs. An early reader who took London to task on this issue was President Theodore Roosevelt.

In 1907, Roosevelt called London and other writers of animal stories "nature-fakers" who confuse the real differences between humans and animals in their fictional accounts. London responded to the President's attack (one has to wonder how the President of the U.S. had enough time for hobbies such as literary criticism while in office!) by arguing that the principles of evolution establish a clear connection or "kinship" between humans and animals.

Similar debates continue, in one form or another, to the present day. Whether one views the dogs as symbols for humans, actual animals, or allegories for philosophers, scientists, historians, or even forms of society will depend largely on the reader. Different critics at various stages of the past century have answered these questions in a number of ways.

The Quest for Mastery

The Call of the Wild links together a number of different obsessive quests, all of which have to do with obtaining a kind of mastery. The Klondike Gold Rush was a pursuit on the part of tens of thousands of people for riches. While London's tale takes place during this event, his work focuses more on the epic struggle for liv-

g creatures (human and animal)
survive the brutality of nature
d natural disasters. Those who
e only in the Yukon in order to
nd gold (Hal, Charles, and
ercedes) fare the worst in the
ot. Meanwhile, the most sympa-
etic characters in *Call* (like
ondon himself)
sire their phys-
al liberty as
ell as their eco-
mic indepen-
nce.

In London's
rsion of mas-
ry in the Wild,
e either mas-
rs the elements
is mastered.
ere is nothing
between and no compromise
ssible. Buck learns while watch-
g Spitz fight Curly that, *He must
aster or be mastered; while to
ow mercy was a weakness.*
ercy did not exist in the primor-
al life. It was misunderstood
r fear, and such misunderstand-
gs make for death. Kill or be
led, eat or be eaten, was the
w; and this mandate, down out
the depths of Time, he obeyed.

The same is true in terms of
astering Nature in the frigid land-
ape. Buck isn't prepared to sur-
ve the cold when he first arrives
Dyea; he has never even *seen*

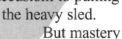

IT HAD NOT TAKEN LONG. TWO MINUTES, PERHAPS, IN ALL BUT THERE LAY CURLY LIMP AND LIFELESS. NO FAIR PLAY. ONCE DOWN, THAT WAS THE END.

snow before! But since he has no
room for failure (death is the out-
come of even a slight misstep),
Buck rapidly makes the transition.
His feet start to harden against the
cold ice, his coat thickens against
the frigid wind, and his muscles
tighten as they accustom to pulling
the heavy sled.

But mastery
in the Wild only
begins with physi-
cal survival. Once
he has adapted to
his surroundings,
Buck begins to
thrive. He chal-
lenges Spitz, in
part, out of his
own need to lead
the pack. He finds
an enjoyment and even an art in the
exhilarating life pursuing basic
needs such as food and sleep. The
author describes Buck's pleasure in
this life in poetic, almost intimate
terms: *There is an ecstasy that
marks the summit of life, and
beyond which life cannot rise. And
such is the paradox of living, this
ecstasy comes when one is most
alive, and it comes as a complete
forgetfulness that one is alive. This
ecstasy, this forgetfulness of living,
comes to the artist, caught up and
out of himself . . . and it came to
Buck, leading the pack . . . . He was
mastered by the sheer surging of*

life, the tidal wave of being, the perfect joy of each separate muscle.

Buck masters his mates in a manner similar to the way that "the sheer surging of life" masters him: utterly and entirely. Attaining mastery over one's fate means a great deal in a world in which life is of little value. London illustrates his somewhat romanticized notion of this world through the cruelty of Hal and Charles as well as the spontaneous dangers of starvation and hypothermia. "As token of what a puppet thing life is," the author provides numerous cases of deaths that the "civilized" world would mourn. But in the Wild, one has to vigilantly maintain whatever mastery one has achieved. Buck cannot drop his guard, even to feel sorry for the loss of Curly or his entire team (after Thornton saves him from Hal) because that would betray signs of mercy and "mercy was a thing reserved for gentler climes."

•Had the author chosen to le John Thornton live, would Buck still leave him (the "ideal maste who had saved his life) for the unknown pack of wolves? Woul you end the story differently? What does the ending of the sto tell you about Buck's character? Does it change how you though of him at the beginning?

•Why does London make Buck the central character of *Th Call of the Wild*? Why doesn't h just use a human character to describe what the dog thinks an feels? Would that change the story? How might London have made Buck not only the central character but the narrator as wel Would that make the story unbe lievable?

Study Questions

•What sort of evolution does Buck experience? How do you understand him to be different at the end of the novel than he is at the beginning? Does Buck's relationship with humans change?

About the Essayist:

Joshua Miller is an Instructor in the Department of English and Comparative Literature at Columbia University. He holds an M.Phil degree from Columbia.